Lincoln

BiG NATE
BLASTS OFF

BALZER + BRAY
An Imprint of HarperCollins*Publishers*

Also by Lincoln Peirce

Big Nate: In a Class by Himself

Big Nate Strikes Again

Big Nate on a Roll

Big Nate Goes for Broke

Big Nate Flips Out

Big Nate: In the Zone

Big Nate Lives It Up

Big Nate: What Could Possibly Go Wrong?

Big Nate: Here Goes Nothing

Big Nate: Genius Mode

Big Nate: Mr. Popularity

Balzer + Bray is an imprint of HarperCollins Publishers.

BIG NATE is a registered trademark of United Feature Syndicate, Inc.

Big Nate Blasts Off

Go to www.bignate.com to read the *Big Nate* comic strip.

Library of Congress Control Number: 2015948269
ISBN 978-0-06-211111-1 (trade bdg.)
ISBN 978-0-06-211112-8 (lib. bdg.)
ISBN 978-0-06-244955-9 (int.)
ISBN 978-0-06-245858-2 (special edition)

Typography by Andrea Vandergrift
16 17 18 19 PC/RRDH 10 9 8 7 6 5 4 3 2 1
❖
First Edition

To David and Phoebe, my champions

You know what's awesome? Social studies.

Yup, you heard me. Social studies is officially the highlight of my day. I like it better than English. And science. And math. I even like it better than ART, which is really saying something . . .

...SINCE I HAPPEN TO BE **NATE WRIGHT**, *ARTISTIC* **GENIUS !**

You're probably thinking: Wait a minute. Hasn't social studies always been a king-size zit on the forehead of life? (Answer: Duh.) So how come it's suddenly jumped to the top of my hot list?

Well, it's NOT because I've magically morphed into a butt-kissing toady like Gina . . .

Even though you didn't **TELL** us to, I read chapter six and answered **ALL** the review questions!

Here! Have some homemade **FUDGE!**

I haven't become a factoid freak like Francis, either.

And it's not like the teaching's gotten any better.

So what's different? Simple answer:

Since dinosaurs roamed the earth, Gina's sat behind me in social studies. I can't prove this, but I'm pretty sure it's Mrs. Godfrey's secret plan for keeping tabs on yours truly.

(It's also given me a nervous twitch, thanks to Gina's psychotic auto-response every time Mrs. Godfrey asks a question. But I digress.)

The point is, Gina's a pain in my backside. So when ol' Dragon Breath decided it was time to shake up the seating arrangements last week, I was totally into it. It couldn't get any worse, right?

WAY right. She moved Gina to the smelliest spot in the room. Welcome to "Death Valley," Needle Nose.

And me? I get to sit in front of Ruby Dinsmore.

I don't know her very well yet, but she seems really nice. She's cute, too. And, best of all, she doesn't go around sucking up to teachers and sticking her report card in your face like Princess Know-It-All.

Gina out, Ruby in. Talk about an upgrade. THAT'S why social studies rocks lately.

"Yeah, I did, too," I say, flipping open my note-book. "Let me find it, and I'll . . . I'll . . . um . . ."

"This? Oh, just a comic book I made," I tell her.

"Really? Can I read it?" Ruby asks.

I hesitate. "It's not . . . I mean, I haven't quite fin-ished it yet, so . . ."

But it IS done. I was just trying to avoid showing it to her, because . . . well, I'll tell you in a minute.

Ruby giggles as she hands back my comic book. "I LIKE it!" she whispers. "And I think I recognize some of these characters!"

Okay . . . but WHICH characters? See, that's why I sort of didn't want her to read it:

 It's not supposed to be realistic or anything; it's just a comic.

But I wouldn't want her to think that I'm, you know, sitting around waiting for her to put a lip-lock on me. Because I'm not. I could have drawn ANYBODY in that last panel. The fact that I drew HER is totally . . . um . . .

Mrs. Godfrey looms over me, nostrils flaring. How does she DO it? The woman's the size of a woolly mammoth on an all-lard diet, but I never hear her coming. She just . . . APPEARS.

"What have you got there?" she demands, peering suspiciously at my comic book. (Quick observation: This isn't going to end well.)

"N-nothing," I stammer, trying to stuff it back into my binder. "Just a project for another class."

Insulting? Excuse me, I just wrote a six-page masterpiece starring HER. You'd think she'd be flattered. But no. She's reaching for her little pink pad. Detention, here I come. Go ahead and stare, everybody. I know you want to.

With one beefy hand, Mrs. Godfrey slams a detention slip down on my desk. "Take this to Mrs. Czerwicki after school," she growls.

Great. It'll be so much fun hanging out with Mrs. Czerwicki again. I haven't seen her since . . . when was it? Oh, yeah:

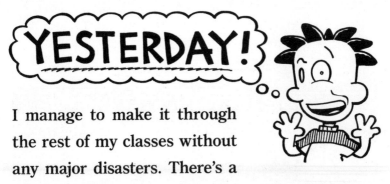

I manage to make it through the rest of my classes without any major disasters. There's a close call in art involving a tube of sky-blue paint, a swivel chair, and Mr. Rosa's pants. Plus, science is a nightmare, because my partner for the lab report is Kim Cressly.

But finally, the bell rings. School's over—for MOST people. I'VE still got an hour to go, thanks to Mrs. Godfrey's total lack of a sense of humor.

I trudge into the detention room, praying that Mrs. Czerwicki's not in one of her complainy moods. The other day, she yakked for forty-five minutes about her varicose veins (whatever those are), and then—

Hey!

CHAPTER 2

Gina—of all people—is standing next to Mrs. Czerwicki's desk. She gives me one of her I'm-better-than-you-are smirks.

Well, let's see. Queen Perfectia has only gotten one detention in her life (for going ballistic in the library—long story), so I doubt she's in any kind of trouble. And sucking up to the detention lady won't score her any precious brownie points. Frankly, I have no clue why she's here.

P.S. 38 TRIVIA! The only person **EVER** to send Gina to detention is the librarian, *MRS. HICKSON!*

Our hero!

"I've got better things to do than to try reading your mind, Gina," I snarl.

She nods. "That's probably just as well . . ."

...SINCE MY MIND IS SO FAR **ABOVE** YOUR READING LEVEL! *SNICKER!*

"Your mind's too SMALL for me to read," I snap.

"That's enough, you two," Mrs. Czerwicki says. "Nate, give me your detention slip."

Correction: I did NOT draw it in class. I just happened to have it WITH me in class. If Mrs. Godfrey's going to stick me in solitary . . .

". . . and spend the next hour THINKING about what you've done!"

Right. That's what she always says. I guess she's hoping something like THIS will happen:

Gross. Let's stop there. Even DRAWING myself hugging it out with ol' Butter Butt would be enough to make me lose my lunch.

Anyway, see what I'm getting at about detention? Adults think it teaches kids all these magical "life lessons," but it just doesn't work that way.

Aaaand away she goes. For someone who's always telling the rest of us not to talk, Mrs. Czerwicki sure can flap her gums. She yaks nonstop until my ears practically start bleeding. Then . . .

"Readers?" I repeat after Gina slithers out of the room. "What's she talking about?"

Mrs. Czerwicki beams. "Gina is writing a profile of me for the next edition of the *Weekly Bugle*!"

Whoops. Didn't mean to sound like I was dissing the *Bugle* there. But, hey, the *Bugle* DESERVES to be dissed. I'll tell you why in a sec. Right now, I've got more important things to take care of.

Ouch. Was that really necessary? I'll admit I get my share of detentions, but it's not like it happens every single day. It's more like two times a week. Or three.

OR... UMMMM... TWELVE.

Never mind. Let's get back to the *Weekly Bugle*. That's the school newspaper, and it's bad.

Not FUNNY bad, like that book Ms. Clarke made us read about the girl raised by dolphins who grew up to become a marine biologist. Just plain old BAD bad. The *Weekly Bugle* has issues.

ISSUE #1: IT'S BORING. We all know that middle schools aren't the most exciting places on earth, but is that any excuse for headlines like these?

NO CHANGES PLANNED TO LUNCH MENU	TOILET IN BOYS' BATHROOM STILL BROKEN
MR. GALVIN "THINKING OF SWITCHING FROM BELT TO SUSPENDERS"	COMPUTER LAB TO GET NEW WASTEBASKET
BOTTLE DRIVE WILL BEGIN SOON	MATH TEAM WINS 3RD PLACE IN TRI-SCHOOL MEET
STUDENT COUNCIL POSTPONES MEETING AGAIN	STUDENT SURVEY: WHAT'S YOUR FAVORITE COLOR?

Note to the *Weekly Bugle* staff: Headlines are supposed to GRAB you, not put you in a coma. If I were in charge, here's what those same headlines would look like:

LUNCH STINKS! STUDENTS' LIVES AT RISK

TIDAL WAVE OF RAW SEWAGE! KIDS TO SCHOOL: STOP "STALL"-ING!

MR. GALVIN ENTERS "FALLING PANTS" ZONE; SANITY QUESTIONED

GARBAGE PILING UP IN COMPUTER LAB! VERMIN ON RAMPAGE!

BOTTLE DRIVE: NOBODY CARES

IT DOESN'T ADD UP: MATH NERDS FINISH LAST

STUDENT COUNCIL EARNS REPUTATION AS DO-NOTHING LOSERS

EXCLUSIVE: WHY DOES *BUGLE* KEEP RUNNING LAME STUDENT SURVEYS?

ISSUE #2: **IT DOESN'T HAVE ANY COMICS.** Or a horoscope, a crossword puzzle, or one of those columns where people write in for advice about how to spice up their putrid marriages. The only attempt to add anything entertaining to the *Bugle* was last month when Maura Flaherty put THIS in:

RIDDLE TIME!!   **By MAURA**

Uh, nice try, Maura. Your "raindrops" look like an invasion of mutant onions. Plus, you're not funny. Want to see how to crack people up? Watch how a REAL cartoonist does it:

By the way, the *Bugle* USED to include my comics. Then a few whiners complained that Dr. Cesspool performing a tonsillectomy with a chain saw was too violent. That was the end of my newspaper career.

ISSUE #3: **THE NAME MAKES NO SENSE.** Here's how Chad put it the other day:

WHY DO THEY CALL IT THE **WEEKLY** BUGLE WHEN IT ONLY COMES OUT ONCE A MONTH?

Exactly. It's so dopey. Maybe they should change the spelling and start calling it the *WEAKLY Bugle*. All I know is . . .

...THE SCHOOL PAPER NEEDS A **MAKEOVER!**

THERE YOU ARE!

HOW WAS DETENTION?

I roll my eyes. "Oh, it was FANTASTIC."

"Imagine Mrs. Czerwicki in a hot tub!" Francis chuckles.

Teddy winces. "Do I have to?"

"What are you guys still doing here?" I ask.

"The Mud Bowl's a long way off," I point out.

"It's never too early to start training!" Teddy answers.

"Hold on, we shouldn't throw a Frisbee inside the building," Francis clucks nervously.

Oh, brother. He can be such a drip. "Stop worrying," I insist. "Nobody'll see us."

With a flick of his wrist, Teddy floats the Frisbee down the corridor. I go charging after it.

ZOW!

I'm at turbo speed, a few feet away from making a highlight reel, top-ten-plays-of-the-century grab, when a door swings open right in front of me.

In an instant, two things are clear: First, I was wrong when I said everyone's gone home. And second, I can't stop.

SLAM!

WHAT ARE YOU DOING, YOU LITTLE TURD?

My vision's a little blurry right now—high-speed collisions have that effect on me—but I recognize that voice. It's Randy Betancourt, winner of P.S. 38's "most likely to mop the floor with someone else's face" award. He grabs a fistful of my shirt and yanks me to my feet.

Wow. If I live through this, today's going straight to the top of my "Worst Days Ever" list. Not only is Randy about to break me in half (or another, even smaller fraction) . . .

CHAPTER 3

All of a sudden, something weird happens. Randy goes from meathead to marshmallow.

"I'm okay . . . ," Ruby answers, looking a little puzzled. "What are you guys doing?"

"Messing around" is one way of putting it. Here's another: HE'S TRYING TO KILL ME.

"Anyway, um, I should probably take off," Randy sputters. Then—and don't say you predicted this, because you didn't—he LETS ME GO!

He doesn't say what kind of stuff, but who cares? If it doesn't involve me losing massive amounts of blood,

I'm all for it. As Randy disappears around the corner, I breathe a huge sigh of relief.

Ruby sort of . . . hesitates. I think she's waiting for me to say something. But this feels different from talking to her in class. This is REAL. I rack my brain for some sort of clever response. Come on, Nate. YOU CAN DO THIS!

Or maybe you CAN'T do this. Nice going, dipwad. Smooth as a sack of sandpaper.

I feel my cheeks getting warm. "Whaddaya mean?"

"Randy!" Teddy answers. "I was sure he was about to PULVERIZE you!"

"Yeah," Francis chimes in.

"He might have thought Ruby would get him in trouble," Teddy suggests. "You know, tell a teacher or something."

Francis is skeptical. "But would that have made him act so un-Randy-like? I doubt it."

Dee Dee appears, looking at the three of us in her boys-are-dumber-than-dirt way.

"Where'd YOU come from?" Teddy asks.

"A great actress never reveals her secrets," she announces. Oh, brother. Did I mention that Dee Dee is the president of the Drama Club?

"I suppose you clowns need me to explain what's going on," she says with a sigh.

Awkward silence. That means yes.

My stomach does a half gainer. Randy likes Ruby?

"Here's MY theory of what happened," Dee Dee goes on. "Randy was about to turn Nate into tofu. . . ."

"He didn't want her to see him acting like a bully! THAT'S why he pretended that he and Nate were just having FUN!"

"Some fun," I grumble.

"Because sometimes," Dee Dee tells us, "boys get flustered when they try to speak to girls!"

I don't answer. Dee Dee obviously saw my epic fail with Ruby back there. Maybe she even suspects that Randy's not the ONLY one with a crush on her. But I'm not ready to go public just yet. It's a secret.

Great. Blabby McBlabb strikes again. Way to broadcast my private life, Dee Dee. What's next, hanging my underwear on the school flagpole?

Anyway, this is big news to Francis and Teddy.

They're right: I've been crazy about Jenny since first grade, and the whole SCHOOL knows that story. But maybe YOU don't. So here it is:

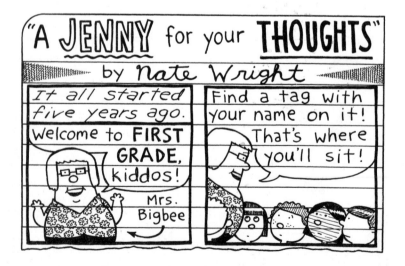

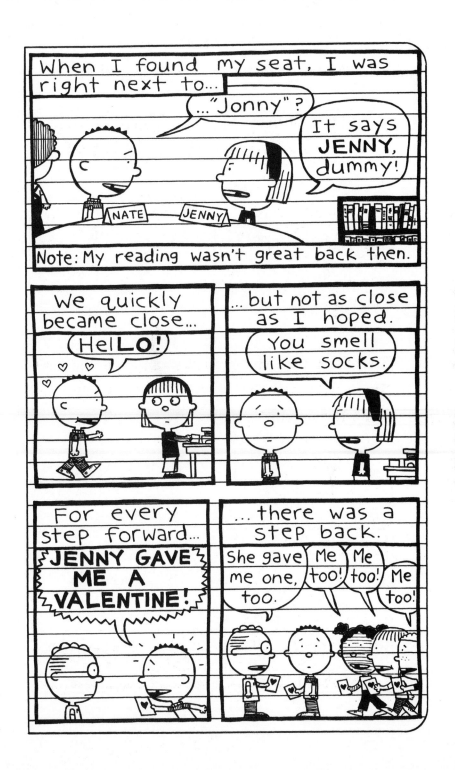

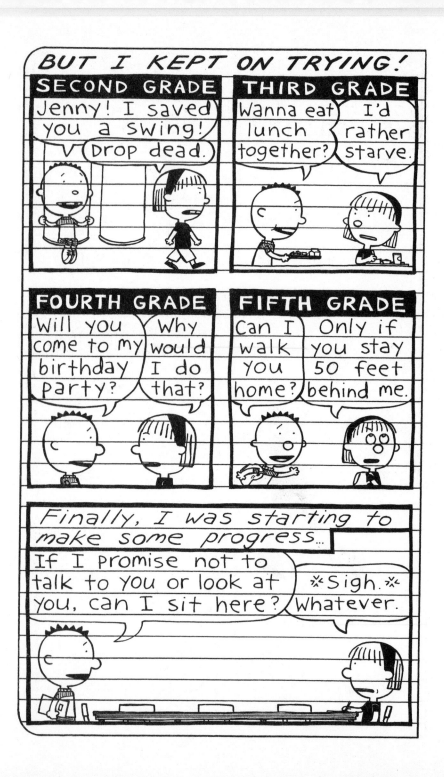

"Until now."

"So you're not in love with Jenny anymore?" Francis sounds stunned. "I don't believe it."

"Believe it," I say simply.

"But WHY, after all this time?" Teddy wonders.

"I don't really know," I admit with a shrug. "But the more I thought about it, the more I realized something."

"What tipped you off, genius?" Teddy cracks. "The five years of constant rejection?"

Francis chuckles. "She's not very nice to you, that's for sure."

"But RUBY is!" Dee Dee chirps. "You two could become the sixth grade's hot new couple!"

"Cut it out, you guys," I tell them. "I barely even KNOW her yet."

Dee Dee snorts. "If Ruby's in love with Randy . . ."

"Don't tell anybody that I like Ruby. I don't want the whole school yakking about it."

"Okay," Dee Dee grumbles. I can tell she's disappointed. Yakking is her life.

"Come on in, guys," I say when we reach my house. We dump our backpacks by the door and pile into the kitchen.

"Anyone for a snack?" Dad asks. There's an uncomfortable silence.

"Um, I think we're gonna go out and toss the Frisbee around," Francis says politely.

"Yeah, gotta practice for the Mud Bowl!" Teddy adds.

Dad's face lights up. "Ah, the Mud Bowl! I was there for the very first one, you know!"

"Really? Did you play in it, Dad?" I ask.

He smiles. "Not only did I play in the Mud Bowl . . ."

CHAPTER 4

Did Dad just say what I thought he said? This might actually be a story worth HEARING!

"Believe it or not . . . ," he begins.

"What were you like back then?" Dee Dee asks in her usual touchy-feely way.

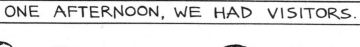
ONE AFTERNOON, WE HAD VISITORS.

IT WAS A BUNCH OF KIDS FROM JEFFERSON MIDDLE SCHOOL — OUR **RIVAL**.

MOVE IT. WE NEED THIS FIELD.

BUT WE WERE HERE **FIRST**!

YEAH, WE'RE PLAYING ULTIMATE!

NO, **WE'RE** PLAYING ULTIMATE!

HEY!

HA HA HAW HAW HA HA

THE JEFFERSON KIDS WERE BIGGER AND STRONGER THAN WE WERE. AND THERE WERE MORE OF THEM, TOO.

THERE WAS NOTHING WE COULD DO.

OR **WAS** THERE?

COME ON, GANG! WE'RE NOT GOING TO TAKE THIS!

WHAT?

MARTY! THOSE GUYS WILL **KILL** US!

I DON'T WANT TO **FIGHT** THEM!

I WANT TO **CHALLENGE** THEM!

I'D NEVER STOOD UP TO A BULLY IN MY LIFE. BUT I JUST COULDN'T LET THOSE JEFFERSON JERKS PUSH US AROUND.

IT WASN'T JUST ABOUT THE FRISBEE. IT WAS FOR **BRAGGING RIGHTS.** P.S. 38 COULD NEVER BEAT JEFFERSON AT **ANYTHING.** THIS WAS OUR CHANCE.

NEWS OF OUR GRUDGE MATCH TRAVELED FAST.

AT THE PARK THE NEXT AFTERNOON, THERE WERE BIG CROWDS FROM BOTH SCHOOLS.

BUT WOULD THERE BE ANYTHING FOR THEM TO WATCH?

UGH. RAIN.

THE FIELD'S TURNING TO **MUD!**

SHOULD WE CALL IT OFF?

WHAT'S **WRONG,** WIMPS? AFRAID OF GETTING **DIRTY?**

WE'RE NOT AFRAID OF **ANYTHING!**

"Interesting fact about mud," Francis notes. "Over time, it hardens into sedimentary rock formations called lutites!"

"WHO CARES?" I shout. "Dad, what happened in the GAME?"

WHO **WON?**

"I'll show you," answers Dad. He rummages through his desk drawer until he finds what he's looking for, then hands me a yellowing piece of paper. "Here's the article from the school newspaper."

BOBCATS BEAF CAVALIERS IN ULTIMATE "MUD BOWL."

"BEAF"?

I THINK IT'S SUPPOSED TO SAY "**BEAT**."

EVEN BACK THEN, THE *WEEKLY BUGLE* WAS TOTALLY USELESS.

READ IT, NATE!

BOBCATS BEAF CAVALIERS IN ULTIMATE "MUD BOWL"

NICNACK PARK—In a severe rainstorm yesterday afternoon, a team of P.S. 38 students overpowered Jefferson Middle School, 13-12, in a super-sensational Ultimate Frisbee game. Because of the soggy, sloppy field, players and fans called this colossal contest the "Mud Bowl."

Marty Wright was the star of the game, making the winning catch during overtime.

From midfield, Simon Birch heaved a 50-yard pass toward the Jefferson end zone. It appeared that it could not be caught, but Wright sprinted past his defender and made an amazing diving grab to win the game. Bobcat fans went totally nuts.

The Jefferson team demanded a rematch, so maybe the Mud Bowl will become an annual event!

Marty Wright, grade 6, makes the winning catch in yesterday's "Mud Bowl" Ultimate Frisbee game against Jefferson.

My jaw just about hits the floor. I stare at Dad in total astonishment.

"I can't believe this!" I continue. "I never knew you were actually GOOD at anything!"

He raises an eyebrow. "Thanks SO much."

Dee Dee's bouncing like a basketball on steroids. "You really DID invent the Mud Bowl!"

Dad nods. "It's nice to have been there at the beginning. Just like the article says, it's become a yearly thing."

"You know what ELSE is tradition? LOSING!" Teddy moans. "P.S. 38 may have won the FIRST Mud Bowl . . ."

Dee Dee speaks up. "Well, if we're going to break that losing streak, we'd better do some practicing!"

We chuck the Frisbee around until it gets dark, and then the gang takes off. After one of Dad's award-winning dinners (and by the way, "chicken fiesta" isn't as fun as it sounds), I head up to my room. I've got a truckload of homework to do. Eventually.

The next morning on the way to school, the guys and I are still talking about the Mud Bowl.

"Here's why we're gonna win," Teddy says. "There have been thirty-seven Mud Bowls, right? That means this NEXT one is number THIRTY-EIGHT!"

"There's no such thing as fate," Francis declares. "Life is a series of random events."

"All I'm saying," Francis goes on, "is that some things are totally out of your control."

Speaking of out of control . . . here comes Dee Dee.

"Why are you acting so weird?" I ask her.

"Me?" she says, putting on her Little Miss Angel face. "I'm NOT! All I'm doing is saying hello!"

There's about ten seconds of radio silence until I can spit out a response. "Wh-what?"

Chad beams at me as he ambles off. "You guys will make a GREAT couple!"

A slow burn starts creeping across my cheeks. Who told CHAD that I like Ruby?

As if I didn't know.

HEH HEH! *ULP!*...
I CAN EXPLAIN!

"Come with me," I snap, and lead Dee Dee into the library so we can talk in private. Not that "private" is part of Dee Dee's vocabulary. I've been annoyed at her before, but this is fifty levels above that. I'm code-red, fire-alarm, butt-sweat MAD.

YOU WERE SUPPOSED TO KEEP YOUR MOUTH SHUT ABOUT RUBY!

I'M SORRY, NATE! I REALLY **AM!**

BOOK NOOK

"I was chatting with a few kids on the way to school, and it just . . . slipped out!"

"Now EVERYBODY'S gonna know!" I hiss.

Dee Dee shakes her head. "No, they're not! I only told Chad and two girls from the Drama Club!"

I glare at Dee Dee. "Got any other predictions?"

She's at a loss for words. There's a first time for everything.

This is a disaster. All I did was tell my best friends that I've got a crush on Ruby. Now—thanks to Dee Dee's motor mouth—it's practically part of the morning announcements. What was it Francis said about stuff happening that you can't control?

CHAPTER 5

So what's my next step? Do I talk to Ruby and explain why half the school thinks we're an item? Do I try to ignore the whole thing?

I'm still peeved at Dee Dee, but one look at her face tells me something's up. And I'm pretty sure it's not a GOOD something. I whirl around.

I guess I should have expected this. Randy was about to massage my nose with his knuckles yesterday, and it didn't happen. Now he wants to finish what he started.

I wait for one of his cheery one-liners—"Prepare to die" is one of his favorites—but he doesn't say a word. He just stands there, looking at me. He doesn't even seem mad. This isn't like Randy. It's kind of creepy.

Slowly, without ever taking his eyes off me, he reaches down, opens up my backpack, and . . .

In an instant, the air is filled with my stuff: notebooks, homework assignments, drawings, you name it. It looks like a ticker tape parade in here—except nobody's celebrating.

Especially not Mrs. Hickson.

Hickey—that's what I call her, but not to her face—
is actually pretty nice. But she goes nuclear if
somebody drops a gum wrapper on the floor, so
you can imagine how thrilled she is with THIS
little scene.

"H-hi, Mrs. Hickson," I stutter, hoping to calm her
down before she unleashes the hounds.

WHO DID THIS?

I turn around to see that
Randy's gone. Typical. He
NEVER gets in trouble.

And he's going to weasel his way out of this one, too. If I tell Hickey it was Randy who carpet bombed the Book Nook, it'll just give him more incentive to kill me. It makes me sick to let him off the hook, but I have no choice. I've got to confess.

"I was . . . um . . . playing a silly joke on Nate, and it got out of hand," Dee Dee lies as I gape at her in shock.

Hickey's surprised, too. And here's the good news: She suddenly looks less mad. "Well . . . the library is no place for playing jokes, you two," she begins.

Phew. As Hickey walks away, I break into a grateful smile. "Thanks, Dee Dee," I say. "You didn't have to take the blame."

"Yes, I did," she answers matter-of-factly.

"Huh? He was still steamed at me for body-slamming him yesterday. How's that YOUR fault?"

"I don't think he's mad about what you did . . ."

"THAT'S the part that's my fault," Dee Dee wails.
She's not being a drama queen. She's really upset.

I can't stay mad at Dee Dee. "It's okay," I tell her.
"He was going to hear about it eventually."

That might be easier said than done, though.
This changes things. Now I'm not just another kid
Randy likes to pick on. I'm COMPETITION. My
stomach lurches as I think about it: I've given him
a reason to really HATE me.

Pleasant thought, right? It rattles around in my head all morning. It's there during social studies . . .

. . . English . . .

. . . and even art.

My so-called best friends aren't exactly helpful.

TGIL: Thank Goodness It's Lunchtime. That means I can focus on something besides Randy . . .

Remember when I told you how bad Dad's snacks are? Well, his lunches are even WORSE. The only way I can get some actual FOOD in me is to find someone crazy enough to trade their lunch for mine.

TODAY'S LUNCH
with **CHEF DAD!**

- *TREASURE OF THE SEA*
Leftover fish casserole served cold, soaked in grease, and lovingly presented in a leaky plastic storage container

- *VEGETABLE MEDLEY*

		Why eat only
← zucchini		**ONE** soggy, over-
← broccoli		cooked veggie when
← cauliflower		you can choke
← unknown		down **FOUR**?

- *OVERRIPE FRUIT DU JOUR*
Today's special: a mealy pear, covered with eye-catching bruises and seeping puncture marks

- *ORGANIC MUFFIN*
Stir one teaspoon of water into two cups of sawdust. Bake until charred and dry.

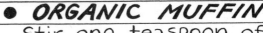

EAT HEARTY!

On the plus side, trying to bargain for something edible is a good way to meet new people. On the minus side . . .

See what I'm up against? Glad I could provide a little comic relief while people are stuffing their faces. Meanwhile, I'm starving to death.

It's Kayla MacIntyre. "Me?" I ask uncertainly. She nods, motioning me over to her table.

YOU KNOW I'M THE EDITOR OF THE *BUGLE*, RIGHT?

Uh, no. What I DO know is that there's a bag of barbecue chips sitting right in front of her. Think she'd trade those for a half-rotten pear?

Kayla obviously hasn't noticed that I'm dying of hunger. "I was in the library earlier when Randy made that major mess," she goes on. "I picked up something I think is yours."

HERE!

AH!

"Yup, this is mine," I confirm.

"Well, I absolutely love it," Kayla tells me. "It's funny, and it's clever, too."

"I know everyone thinks the *Bugle* stinks," she continues, reading my mind, "but I'm trying to change that! We need more people to get involved!"

"Involved how?"

"But . . . what would I write about?"

"It wouldn't just be writing," she explains. "You can add drawings, too! That's what'll make it unique!"

I flinch. GOSSIP isn't exactly my favorite word since the news that I like Ruby went viral. But if I'm the one writing the column . . .

I zip over to our regular table and tell Francis and Teddy the big news. "Pretty cool, right?" I say after giving them all the details.

"But you're always complaining about how horrible the *Bugle* is," Francis points out.

"What are you going to call it?" Teddy asks.

"I've got the perfect title!" Francis announces.

"Hey, I LIKE that!" I exclaim.

WHEN SOMETHING'S A **BLAST**, THAT MEANS IT'S **FUN**!

RIGHT! AND A **BLAST** IS ALSO THE SOUND A **BUGLE** MAKES!

COOL!

"It's an awesome name," Teddy agrees. "What's going to be the subject of your first column?"

"I'm not sure. Maybe some sort of list."

LIKE "P.S. 38'S BEST COUPLES" OR SOMETHING LIKE THAT!

HI, NATE!

RUBY! HI!

SPEAKING OF COUPLES...

"I heard you have a really awful lunch today." She giggles.

I respond with what's supposed to be a charming laugh, but it ends up sounding like a bizarre burp-hiccup combo. "Uh . . . yeah," I finally manage to say. "My dad's clueless about lunches."

"Hey, HEY!" Teddy grins after Ruby's out of earshot. "That's a good sign!"

Francis bobs his head in agreement. "Yeah, Nate! She wouldn't give you a soda if she didn't like you!"

My heart pounds. Maybe he's right. I mean, she did sort of make an effort to be nice to me. What does it mean? My brain swirls with thoughts of Ruby as I gaze at the can and pop it open.

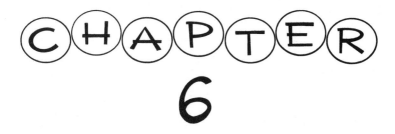

CHAPTER 6

Twelve ounces of root beer explode in my face.
I drop the can, but the damage is done: I'm soaked.
Nothing like taking a soda shower in front of a
few hundred people.

Francis and Teddy know not to laugh. They bust my chops about lots of stuff—best friends are SUPPOSED to do that—but they can tell this isn't your everyday awkward moment. This feels . . .

Leave it to Francis to have a bunch of extra napkins in his lunch bag. As I mop myself off, Teddy gets right to the point:

I nod miserably. "I know."

"What are you saying?" Francis asks.

Teddy shrugs. "I'm saying that Ruby must have booby-trapped the can."

"What? That makes no SENSE!" Francis sputters.

DIDN'T WE ALL JUST AGREE THAT RUBY **LIKES** NATE?

"Well . . . we THOUGHT she did," I mutter. My stomach twists into a clammy knot. I wish I could disappear.

Francis shakes his head. "This is illogical," he says like he's analyzing a science project gone wrong. "Why would Ruby act so nice . . ."

. . .AND THEN DO SOME-THING SO **MEAN?**

SHE **WOULDN'T!**

"I saw the whole thing," Dee Dee announces. "It wasn't Ruby's fault!"

HERE'S WHAT HAPPENED!

RUBY WAS JUST FINISHING HER LUNCH WHEN ARTUR WALKED BY.

CLEAN UP PLEASE

ACH. POOR NATE.

HUH? WHY POOR NATE?

HE IS TRY TO TRADE WITH SOMEONE HIS BAD LUNCH!

BUT IT IS NOT GO VERY GOOD, I THINK.

AW! THAT'S SO **SAD**!

EW.

I HAVEN'T HAD MY ROOT BEER YET...

DO YOU THINK NATE MIGHT WANT IT?

OH, YES! DEFINITE!

!

RUBY LEFT THE CAN ON THE TABLE AND WENT TO THROW AWAY HER LUNCH GARBAGE...

...AND THAT'S WHEN I REALIZED I WASN'T THE **ONLY** ONE WHO'D BEEN LISTENING!

RANDY SHOOK UP THE CAN WHILE RUBY WASN'T LOOKING...

SHOOF
SHOOF
SHOOF
SHOOF
SHOOF
SHOOF

...AND THEN OFF SHE WENT TO GIVE IT TO **YOU!**

I feel a jolt of energy go through me. So this was all RANDY'S doing! I should've known. Ruby wouldn't punk me like that. Dee Dee's detective work just proved it.

"You saw Randy rig the can to explode! Why didn't you stop Ruby from giving it to Nate?"

Exactly! If Dee Dee had said something, I could have avoided getting a root beer facial.

"I TRIED!" Dee Dee insists. "I was about to run over here . . ."

Ah-ha. Mrs. Colletti's the lunch aide, and when she tells you to clean up, you clean up. She's sort of like Coach John, but with hairier legs.

"We'll do it, Nate," Dee Dee offers.

YOU GO WASH YOUR**SELF** OFF!

Good idea. Francis's napkins helped, but I'm still wearing about half a can of root beer. And it's starting to dry into a sticky film. I feel like a candy cane that's been licked all over.

I leave the cafetorium, head for the bathroom . . .

BOYS

. . . and stumble into a meeting of the Hate Nate Club. President Randy Betancourt presiding.

"As if you didn't know," I growl.

"Sorry," Randy says with a smirk, "but I have no idea what you're talking about." His gruesome groupies snicker on cue.

A look of uncertainty flickers across his face, but he recovers quickly. Randy turns to the rest of his gang. "Get lost, you guys," he barks.

The door closes behind them. One second later, Randy's in my face. "You keep your mouth shut about Ruby," he snarls.

I'm pretty sure he's about to smack me, but at this point I'm more mad than scared. I take a deep breath. "I just think it's a weird way to show a girl you like her . . ."

...BY TRICKING HER INTO DOING YOUR DIRTY WORK!

Randy's eyes flash angrily, and he bares his teeth like a rabid dog. Uh, remember that "more mad than scared" comment? Forget that—I'm terrified.

Then in walks the sheriff.

Just so you know: You're witnessing a miracle. Principal Nichols NEVER shows up when I need him. His specialty is showing up when I DON'T.

"I'll ask again," the Big Guy thunders. "What's going on here?"

Before I can answer, Randy shifts smoothly into his Mr. Innocent act. "I was just using the bathroom," he begins.

THEN **NATE** BARGED IN AND STARTED **YELLING** AT ME!

"Yes," Principal Nichols agrees as he strokes his chin. "I DID hear shouting."

EXPLAIN YOURSELF, NATE!

WHY WERE YOU YELLING AT RANDY?

Do I really need to tell you what happens next? Randy waltzes back to his posse of pinheads, while Principal Nichols gives me a five-star butt chewing.

"Are you sending me to detention?" I ask.

He ushers me into the hallway. "I don't think detention's the answer in this case. It doesn't seem to have kept you from picking on Randy."

Yes, okay, we've clashed . . . BECAUSE HE'S A PSYCHO! Is it just P.S. 38, or do all schools have principals this clueless?

"If you can't stay out of Randy's way, Nate . . ."

Gulp. Wonder what THAT meant. I'm no fan of detention, but it's probably a cakewalk compared to anything Nichols could come up with.

My thoughts turn back to Randy. This is totally his fault. What a . . .

...SCUZZBALL
...BONEHEAD
...DIPWAD
...JERK

...BUTT NUGGET
...DOORKNOB
...NOSEWIPE
...TOOLBOX

I'm going with "all of the above." And if I come up with any more nasty names—dirtbag, anyone?—I'll add them to the list.

The rest of the day isn't much fun. Randy's in all my afternoon classes, so there's no way to avoid him. He's still feeling pretty good about himself thanks to that soda can episode.

✳SNIFF! SNIFF!✳

I SMELL ROOT BEER!

He's trying to tick me off—that's obvious. He's hoping I'll snap, have some mega meltdown, and get in more trouble. But I'm not going to give him what he wants.

No, I'm not gonna get mad.

CHAPTER 7

After school, I head straight home. No listening to Mrs. Czerwicki complain about her chronic foot fungus. No practicing for the Mud Bowl.

Correction: I WILL be on a mission once Dad moves his double-wide out of the way.

Hmm. Dad's not wearing his usual duds from the Big & Tacky rack at Bargain Barn. "How come you're all dressed up?" I ask.

"Oh, it's just a work thing," he says. "No big deal."

"How about bringing home a pizza, Dad?" I suggest. "We haven't eaten takeout in—"

He cuts me off. "No takeout.

I'll make dinner for us later."

Oh, goody. I can't wait.

(Not-so-fun fact: Baloney bubbles are just plain old fried baloney. Dad started calling it that when we were little to make it sound less pathetic.)

"That's strange," Ellen says after Dad leaves.

True. Dad's got one of those jobs where he works from home half the time, and he dresses pretty casual around the house. I mean, he spent yesterday in a pair of boxers and a BALD IS BEAUTIFUL

T-shirt. So it's weird to see him decked out like your friendly neighborhood mannequin.

FYI, Gordie is Ellen's boyfriend. And, yes, that DOES call his mental stability into question. But you can tell he's got all his marbles because he works at Klassic Komix in the mall. Comics Store Employee is # 5 on my list of all-time dream jobs. Here are the top four:

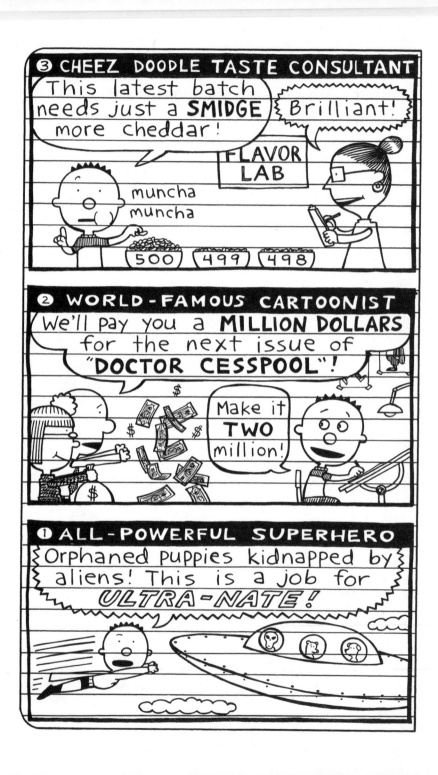

"I wish you DID have Gordie's job," Ellen grouses. "It's our six-month anniversary this weekend, and he has to WORK."

"Wow," I say. "You guys have been going out for six months?" Not that I really care, but give me a minute here. This is research.

Ellen's eyes light up, and she flashes one of her obnoxious grins. "You LIKE somebody!"

"Shut up," I snap, my cheeks burning. "I was just making conversation, that's all. Never mind."

"Oh, come on, Romeo. Who's the unlucky girl? Are you still hung up on what's her face? Jenny?"

Ellen scowls. "Hey, don't bite MY head off! YOU'RE the one who brought it up!"

She stalks off, which is fine with me. Big sisters are such a waste of oxygen. Meanwhile, I'm still pretty confused about this whole Ruby situation.

| I know I like her. | But does she like me? . . . | Or does she like Randy? |

Ugh. Suddenly, a picture of Randy and Ruby smooching in slow motion flashes through my mind. It's sickening, but it's just what I needed. It helps me focus on the job at hand:

The next morning before homeroom, I find Kayla in the library.

. . . And wait. And wait some more. Remember, this is the (ha-ha) *"Weekly" Bugle.* It's actually almost TWO weeks before the next issue—featuring the awesome debut of yours truly—finally comes out.

READ ALL ABOUT IT!

Let's skip Gina's thrilling profile of Mrs. Czerwicki (with the headline DETENTION MONITOR KEEPS WORKING DESPITE MYSTERIOUS SKIN RASH) and go straight to the main attraction:

VOL. 1 ★ ★ ★ ★ ★ ★ NO. 1

BUGLE BLASTS!

By NATE WRIGHT

"All the news that fits... I print!"

Greetings, readers! Welcome to a NEW column that will keep you PLUGGED IN to all the latest news at P.S. 38! Let's get started with an exclusive...

ROMANCE REPORT!

Derek and Melissa have eaten lunch together for three straight days! Everyone's wondering: Is LOVE on the menu?

TELLTALE SIGN: THEY'RE FEEDING EACH OTHER!

A loud argument between **Austin and Lucy** in the Book Nook meant two things:

Overheard on Monday near the science lab: **Bethany** drops an f-bomb on **Leo**.

Overheard on Tuesday by the trophy case: Leo bounces back quickly.

TIME FOR...
TEACHER TIDBITS!

How well do **YOU** know the members of P.S. 38's faculty? These facts will **AMAZE** you!

A certain social studies teacher loves horseback riding (which leads to the question: Is the horse okay?).

This fossilized science instructor once tried a perm (back when he actually had hair). Talk about a failed experiment!

A psychotic employee of the phys ed department is currently undergoing treatment for "chronic flatulence."

And now it's time to play...

GUESS THAT GUY!

USE THESE FIVE CLUES TO UNMASK THE MYSTERY STUDENT!

1. He's not the sharpest tool in the shed.

2. His nose is HUMONGOUS.

3. He has really, really bad breath.

4. He's always picking on smaller kids.

❺ He is a TOTAL WEASEL!

BONUS CLUE: Our mystery student's name rhymes with "Shmandy Shmetancourt."

★   ★   ★   ★   ★   ★   ★

That's all for this time! Read the next edition of the *Weekly Bugle* for another installment of **BUGLE BLASTS!**

I can tell right away I've got a hit on my hands.

The hallways are packed with kids reading the *Bugle,* and they're all cracking up. I'm getting high fives all over the place. Even from Leo.

Did you hear that? That's the best part: People love that I called out Randy. The principal might not realize what he's really like, but the KIDS do.

I'm not stupid. I knew that as soon as Randy saw "Bugle Blasts," he'd go completely scooters. But I guess I just reached the end of my rope. He's been doing the same garbage for so long—and NEVER taking the blame for it—that I finally decided to fight back. (Of course, I was hoping to avoid any actual fighting. No such luck.)

Principal Nichols shows up about two minutes too late, as usual. And right away, Randy launches into his "I'm a victim" act.

It's Ms. Dempsey, the school counselor. Without taking her eyes off Randy, she leans in close to the principal and whispers something. He listens, nods a couple times, and turns toward us.

BOYS, GO TO MY OFFICE AND WAIT FOR ME THERE.

Five minutes later, the Big Guy is parked behind his desk, giving us both the evil eye.

LET'S START WITH YOU, RANDY.

WOULD YOU LIKE TO CHANGE YOUR ACCOUNT OF HOW THE FIGHT STARTED?

Randy shoots me a murderous glance before mumbling, "I jumped on him."

"Mm-hmm. Yes, that confirms what Ms. Dempsey told me," Principal Nichols says. "And Nate . . . what do you suppose made Randy angry enough to assault you that way?"

There's a copy of the *Weekly Bugle* right there on his desk. It's no use playing dumb.

I...UH... MADE FUN OF HIM IN THE NEWSPAPER.

"In other words," Principal Nichols concludes, "BOTH of you bear some responsibility for this problem."

...WHICH MEANS YOU SHOULD BOTH PLAY A PART IN THE **SOLUTION!**

Uh, what's THAT supposed to mean? Please tell me he's not talking about one of those stupid "team building" activities they make us do every year on the first day of school.

"Ms. Dempsey has suggested that the two of you try peer counseling," Principal Nichols tells us.

"Sometimes a fellow STUDENT is better at solving these sorts of disputes than an ADULT is," he explains.

Randy looks as thrilled about this as I am. "You mean we have to tell some student shrink why we hate each other?"

Principal Nichols smiles. Or grimaces. Hard to tell which. "Something like that," he says.

He presses the intercom button on his desk. "Mrs. Shipulski," he says . . .

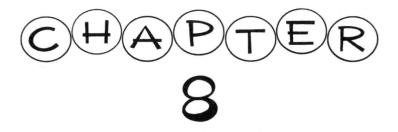

CHAPTER 8

Please let it be someone good. Please let it be someone good. Please let it—

Principal Nichols glares at me, and there's an edge to his voice. "Is something WRONG, Nate?"

Wrong? Oh, you mean like finding out my peer counselor is the BRIDE OF FRANKENSTEIN??

"The three of you will meet after school today to begin a dialogue," he explains.

A dialogue. Great. I can hear it now:

"Gina's gone through the counselor training," Principal Nichols says. "SHE'LL be in charge."

Ugh. This is awful. I've had bad dreams before . . .

. . . But this is no dream. It's as real as a boot in the backside. And just as enjoyable.

Principal Nichols wraps up his instructions. Gina and Randy walk out, but before I can make my escape, the Big Guy pounces.

JUST A MOMENT, NATE. WE'RE NOT QUITE DONE.

I swallow hard. NOW what?

He points to his copy of the *Bugle*. "In your column, you did more than take potshots at Randy. You also poked fun at some TEACHERS in a way that crossed the line."

My mouth goes dry. "Well . . . yeah . . . but I didn't mention any of them by NAME!"

BUT YOU WERE PRETTY CLEAR ABOUT WHICH TEACHERS YOU MEANT!...

...WEREN'T YOU?

"Uh-huh," I murmur, looking at the floor.

There's a long silence. "Nate, you're a talented cartoonist. It's wonderful that you're so skilled at using humor to express yourself."

Wait for it. Here it comes. He's going to suspend me, or put me on probation, or . . .

My head's spinning as I shuffle
out. I've got the usual queasiness
I always feel after a shame-a-thon
with the principal . . .

. . . But I have to admit, I'm still kind of pumped
by all the rave reviews for "Bugle Blasts." If everyone keeps telling me how awesome I am . . .

Francis scowls. "We just heard you've got peer counseling after school."

"Don't remind me," I grumble.

Oops. I forgot about Mud Bowl practice.

"Not only that," Teddy adds, "you're missing a chance to hang out with your DREAM GIRL."

My stomach sinks like a brick in a bathtub. I'm starting to feel like the dope who guesses wrong on one of those TV game shows.

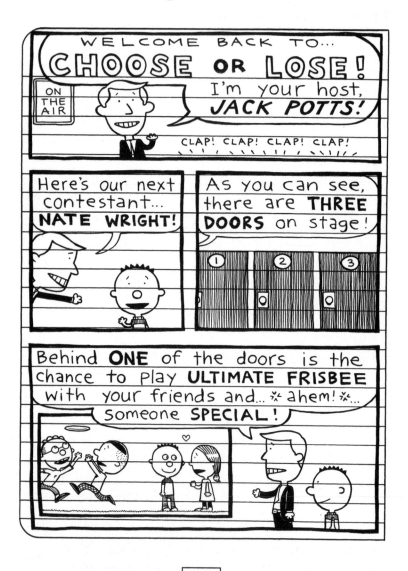

I try not to think about it. But there's a clock in every classroom, and each tick brings me one second closer to couples therapy with Gina and Randy. It's a countdown to misery, until . . .

She looks puzzled. "But I thought the two of you were FRIENDS. Remember that day I saw you and him wrestling, and—"

". . . And Randy said we were just messing around?" I say. "Yeah, I remember. But we're not friends."

I hesitate. I don't really want to tell Ruby about all the times Randy's punked me over the years. That'll make me sound like Wee Willie Weenie.

Instead, I pull a copy of the newspaper out of my notebook and flip it open to "Bugle Blasts."

I roll my eyes. "He's ALWAYS mad at me. But this definitely kicked it up a notch."

Ruby shrugs. "He never seems mad around ME."

Whoa, what's THAT supposed to mean? Is she sending me some sort of coded message?

Rats. So much for THAT conversation. It's time for science, and Ruby and I are stuck at different lab stations for the whole period. I try to catch up with her after class, but . . .

Remember what Principal Nichols said? Gina's in charge. And she knows it, too. Gag me.

Fine. But I'm not gonna be EARLY, either. As I stroll leisurely downstairs, I spot the Mud Bowl team heading off to practice.

They don't answer. Guess they couldn't hear me. Trying to ignore the hollow feeling in my chest, I slip into Ms. Dempsey's office. Gina and Randy are already there.

"This is stupid," Randy mutters under his breath. For once, he and I agree about something.

Wait, did he say . . . MORE counseling?

Gina ignores him. "Let's get started," she says briskly, handing us paper and pencil. "I'd like each of you to record your impressions of one another."

"Impressions?" Randy repeats. (Did I mention he's not very bright?)

Sounds easy enough, right? Well, not really. It's no problem listing all the bad stuff . . .

. . . but how am I supposed to write about Randy's GOOD qualities?

"Uh . . . hold it," I protest. "I'm not done."

"Sorry," Gina says, managing to sound not sorry at all. "We're on a schedule."

She collects our sheets and examines them briefly.

"Now you'll exchange papers," Gina announces. She hands mine to Randy, and his to me.

CHAPTER 9

As I stare at the page, the blood starts pounding in my head. I can't believe what I'm seeing.

"You look upset," Gina says, a smirk tugging at the corners of her mouth. "Is something wrong?"

"YES, something's wrong! . . ."

"Is this a joke?" I snarl at Randy.

He grins. "You tell me."

"I don't think it's funny."

His face twists into a mask of bogus concern.

I search for a snappy comeback but can't find one.

Randy points at the drawing in my hand. "What if I put that cartoon in the *Bugle* for the whole school to see? And what if I gave it a clever TITLE? . . ."

This isn't fair. He's acting like I drew "Guess That Guy" for no reason. "I only did that because you were such a jerk," I protest.

"I'm a jerk to you because you're a jerk to me."

"We're getting nowhere," Gina declares in full know-it-all mode. "Let's try something else."

So we do. We try EVERYTHING:

Nothing works. By the end of the session, two things are obvious: (1) I can't believe I missed Mud Bowl practice for this, and (2) Randy and I still hate each other.

No kidding, genius. The whole sixth grade is going to the science museum. What does that have to do with peer counseling?

"Mr. Galvin always makes kids pair up on field trips," Gina explains.

Randy's as horrified as I am, but what can we do? Thanks to Principal Nichols, Gina's calling all the shots.

I just remembered: I haven't asked Dad to sign the permission slip for the field trip yet. Do I want to be Randy's partner? No. But would I rather skip the field trip altogether? No WAY. Staying at school during field trips means spending the day with Mrs. Jones, aka Mrs. Drones.

I can see the headline now: STUDENT BORED TO DEATH BY CLASSROOM AIDE. I make sure the permission slip's in my backpack, and start home.

"Uh, hold it," I say, pointing to a blank space. "You need to fill in your phone number at work."

"I wrote down our home phone," he says.

"Yeah, but the field trip is on a Wednesday, and you always go to the office on Wednesdays, so . . ."

My voice trails off as I look at Dad. He's got an expression on his face that's . . . well, I don't know WHAT it is. I've never seen that face before.

Family meetings are either really good or really bad . . . and Dad wasn't smiling back there. As I enter Ellen's room, an alien world of strawberry lip gloss and stuffed panda bears,

I feel a cold knot forming in my belly. Something's not right.

"Sit down," Dad says, motioning to the sofa.

Ellen sits; I don't. I'm too nervous.

Dad clears his throat. "I've been trying to figure out how to say this, but there's no easy way. So

I'll just go ahead and tell you."

Wait, this doesn't add up. "Last MONTH?" I say. "But we saw you going to the office just a couple WEEKS ago!"

"I've been going to LOTS of interviews lately," Dad continues, "trying to find a job locally. Staying here would be my first choice."

"First choice?" Ellen echoes, her voice sounding thin. "W-what's the SECOND choice?"

Dad takes a deep breath. "Well, there IS a company that wants to hire me . . ."

...IN **CALIFORNIA.**

It feels like all the air's left the room.

"California?" I repeat.

"So . . . we're moving?" Ellen whispers.

Dad smiles. Saddest smile ever. "Unless I can find work here in town . . ."

YES, HONEY. I'M AFRAID WE'LL HAVE TO.

Ellen turns and runs out of the room. I hear her feet thundering up the stairs, her door slamming, the floor creaking as she throws herself onto her bed. I can tell she's crying into her pillow, because I recognize the sound. It's like a humpback whale having an asthma attack.

I look at Dad. "You could still find a job around here, though. Right? I mean . . ."

"I suppose so," he answers quietly. Then his voice takes a U-turn, suddenly all fake cheer and confidence. "We'll be okay. No matter what happens, I promise it'll be okay."

He goes into the kitchen to burn dinner. I wander outside and collapse on the lawn. Did you hear how he put that? NO MATTER WHAT HAPPENS.

"Hey, tell us about peer counseling!" Dee Dee says as the gang flops down beside me.

"Yeah, give us details!" Teddy chimes in.

"It was fine," I mumble.

I shake my head. "Nothing. Everything's good."

I know what you're thinking: These are my best friends, so why not tell them I might be moving three thousand miles away? I can't really explain it. I know they'd all try to make me feel better . . .

California is FASCINATING, meteorogically speaking! The average temperature is...	In a few years, after I become a STAR in Hollywood, we can be NEIGHBORS!!	Here's a JOKE that'll cheer you up! A duck walks into a barber shop...

. . . but what if I'm not READY to feel better? I only found out about this California plan two minutes ago. The last thing I want to do is TALK about it. So I won't. I'll change the subject.

"How was practice?" I ask.

"She said you're really nice, and she loves your sense of humor! She thinks you're cute, too! She even likes your HAIR!"

"So this girl is literally one in a million," Teddy cracks. Everyone laughs. Except me.

I guess this is why people say timing is everything. Yesterday I would have been ecstatic to learn that Ruby likes me. But now . . .

Francis elbows me in the ribs. "Well? When are you going to ask her out?"

I get to my feet. "I'm not."

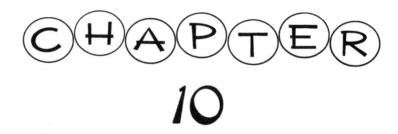

CHAPTER 10

"What's WITH you lately, Nate?" Francis asks as we arrive at school on Wednesday morning.

Dee Dee's half right. The field trip IS today, but Randy's barely a blip on my radar screen. Besides, soon he'll be out of my life forever.

...ALONG WITH EVERYONE ELSE.

ALL SIXTH GRADERS... REPORT TO THE BUS CIRCLE FOR THE TRIP TO THE SCIENCE MUSEUM.

I still haven't told anybody I'm moving. I guess I'm hoping for a last-minute miracle. But Dad's only got one more job interview lined up. If that doesn't pan out . . .

CALIFORNIA, HERE I COME.

I spot Ruby up ahead as we board the bus, and my insides go into a death spiral. Obviously, I was lying when I said I'd changed my mind about her.

I still think she's awesome. But what's the point of telling her how I feel . . .

It's a twenty-minute ride to the museum, but thanks to Mary Ellen Popowski, it seems longer.

Finally, we pull up to the entrance and stream into the lobby. And even though I'm in a cruddy mood, this DOES look like a cool place to roam around . . .

. . . until Captain Killjoy drops a turd in the punch bowl. "No goofing off," Mr. Galvin announces. "We're here to LEARN." We all groan. Why are teachers always so hung up on LEARNING stuff?

"You heard the man," Gina insists, steering me toward Randy.

He and I exchange angry glares. "Let's get this over with," he grunts. "Where do we go first?"

I glance at the booklet. "The entomology exhibit. Entomology is the study of insects."

"I know what entomology is," Randy gripes. "I'm not an idiot."

"You handle that part," he tells me.

That's so Randy—trying to weasel out of doing any work. "Why ME? Why don't YOU do it?"

Wait, did that sound like I was thanking Randy for calling me a pinhead? Because that's not what I meant. I think I was just in shock that he paid me a compliment . . . sort of.

He scans the booklet. "There's a jillion questions in here. If we split up, it'll go faster."

He wanders off, and I take the elevator up to Entomology. I find the titan beetle in a glass display case and start drawing.

Hey, this gives me an idea for my next "Ultra-Nate" comic:

The elevator opens, and a bunch of students pour out. They're not from P.S. 38, though, so I don't pay much attention as the group files past. Then something grabs my attention.

One of the kids is wearing a familiar jacket. Purple and gold, with a big *J* on the chest.

J... FOR JEFFERSON!

Ugh. It figures. We go on one stinkin' field trip a year, and the Evil Empire is here on the same day. I give them a subtle (but still devastating) hairy eyeball as they file past. They're too busy being obnoxious to notice. I turn back to my drawing.

Uh-oh. It's Nolan.

We've crossed paths before. During the winter, when P.S. 38 had to relocate to Jefferson for a while, he wasn't exactly driving the welcome wagon. Now here he is again, as friendly as ever.

"Give that back," I demand.

He ignores me and stuffs it in his pocket.

"So what if I am?" I answer, trying not to focus on the fact that he's about a foot taller than me.

He pokes me hard in the chest. "We're going to DESTROY you."

His face darkens. "You're going down," he hisses. "Not just in the Mud Bowl . . ."

"Why should I?" Nolan sneers.

"Do the math," Randy says matter-of-factly. "There's only one of you . . ."

Okay, am I the only one who thinks this is bizarre? Randy Betancourt, P.S. 38's poster boy for bullying, IS STICKING UP FOR ME! And you know what? It's working. Nolan starts to inch away.

"Two against one," he sputters. "Real fair."

"Huh," I say, finding my voice again. "Funny how you're worried about fairness all of a sudden."

Nolan disappears. I knock the dust off my clothes and turn to Randy.

He waves me away impatiently. "Whatever. The guy's a scumbag."

I spot my pencil on the floor and, with a groan, remember the booklet.

Randy slumps onto a nearby bench. "So we'll get an F. Great. That's just what I need."

"Counselor? You mean Ms. Dempsey?"

His cheeks turn a blotchy pink. "Never mind. It's none of your business."

"How come you go to counseling?"

His voice is expressionless. "Because my grades stink. And my parents are getting a divorce. So there. Shut up."

Randy looks miserable. I should probably keep quiet, but I feel something working its way from my lungs to my throat to my mouth. I can't stop it. All of a sudden, my voice has a mind of its own.

I THINK I'M MOVING TO CALIFORNIA.

Randy can't hide his surprise. "You are?"

I nod. "My father says it's not a hundred percent . . ."

He frowns. "It's no fun, I can tell you that."

"Huh? When have YOU ever moved?"

"I move every WEEK," he says, spitting out the words as he rises from the bench.

I'm no counselor, but something tells me now's a good time to leave Randy alone. I zip down to the lobby, and it turns out Mr. Galvin DOES have some extra booklets. I have to run around like my undies are on fire, but I finish page one just before it's time to leave. So Randy and I won't get an F. Or an A, either, based on this beetle drawing.

Mary Ellen tries to get another round of campfire songs going during the trip back to school, but I'm focusing on the Mud Bowl. It could be the last game I ever play as a Bobcat, and . . .

I shake my head. "No, but last year they beat us twenty-five to six, remember?"

"And they were big," Teddy adds. "They had some kids who could throw that disk a MILE."

"That's what OUR team needs," I say as the bus slows to a stop in front of P.S. 38.

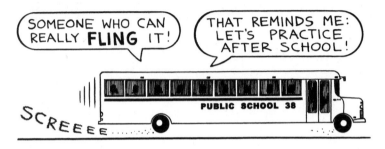

"You don't have peer counseling again, do you?" Teddy asks me.

A few minutes later, the battlin' Bobcats are out on the soccer field: Francis, Teddy, Dee Dee, Chad . . .

. . . and Ruby. And me. Awkward.

Yeah, really fun. Except for the part where Nolan tossed me around like a sock puppet.

Teddy launches a disk in my direction, but the wind catches it. It banks to the left, farther and farther off course, until . . .

With an expert flick of the wrist, Randy sends the disk my way. It doesn't wobble. It doesn't curve. I don't even have to move. I just hold up my hands.

It's a perfect throw. PERFECT. It's exactly the kind of throw Jefferson can make. And we can't.

I don't hesitate. I sprint over to Randy. I can't believe I'm asking this, but . . .

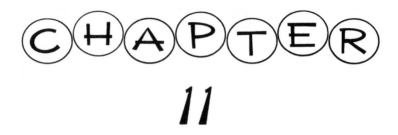

CHAPTER
11

"Let me get this straight," Francis whispers.

"WHY?" Teddy chimes in. "You spend a couple hours with the guy on a field trip, and all of a sudden you're best friends?"

"We're not best friends," I assure them.

On the Skept-O-Meter, they're giving me looks that are somewhere between *I'm not so sure about this* and *You're out of your mind*. But finally, Francis caves. "Well," he sighs. "I guess we can try it."

Just your everyday epic plot twist. A week ago, Randy wanted to pound my face in. Now we're teammates. It's kind of freaky. But asking him to join us seems like a win-win. He gets to take his mind off his parents' divorce, and we increase our chances of winning the Mud Bowl.

That's assuming we even GET to the Mud Bowl. We have to survive PRACTICE first. After just a few minutes, I can see that having Randy on the team will definitely take some getting used to.

Francis and I are taking a water break when Dee Dee joins us. "I couldn't help but notice that Randy's making all his most acrobatic plays right in front of Ruby," she mutters under her breath.

"Yeah," I grumble. "He sure is."

"Well, what do YOU care?" Francis asks me.

"Oh . . . uh . . . I don't," I stammer. "I was just . . . you know . . . watching Randy do his thing."

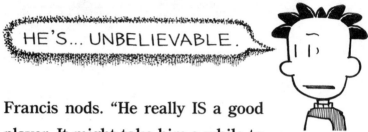

HE'S... UNBELIEVABLE.

Francis nods. "He really IS a good player. It might take him a while to fit in, but I think you were right . . ."

HE'LL HELP US AGAINST JEFFERSON!

C'MON, LET'S GET BACK OUT THERE!

UH... NATE AND I WILL BE ALONG IN A SECOND.

Francis trots onto the field. Dee Dee waits until he's out of earshot. "You can fool everyone else," she declares, poking my shoulder. "But not me."

"What are you talking about?"

Dramatic sigh. Huge eye roll. "I'm talking about this ACT you're putting on."

190

I try to avoid eye contact. Dee Dee's not easy to lie to. "I have my reasons."

"But if you both like each other, why—"

"Just leave it alone, okay?"

Whoops. Probably shouldn't have gone there. Dee Dee pounces like Chad on a cupcake.

"Next week? What do you mean? What's happening next week?"

She's not going to let this go. And you know what? I'm not sure I WANT her to. I've been keeping this bottled up long enough. Maybe it's time to finally say something.

I take a deep breath.

Huh. What's Dad doing here? He NEVER picks me up at school. "Um . . . I'll be right back," I tell Dee Dee as I jog over to the car.

Dad greets me with a smile. "How was the science museum?" he asks.

"Fine," I answer. But, come on—he didn't drive here to quiz me about a stinkin' field trip.

A sickening layer of dread settles over me. So it's official. My mouth goes bone-dry as I confirm the horrible news. "The . . . the one in California?"

HERE... IN... TOWN!

Dad's still talking. "Remember how I still had one interview left? Well, it was this morning, and—"

"So we're not moving?" Sorry, I know it's rude to interrupt. But I've got to hear Dad say it. Just to be sure.

He chuckles. "We're not moving."

WOO HOO HOO HOOOOOOOOOoo

I'M NOT MOVING!!

WHAM!

I... AM... NOT... MOVING!!

THAT'S GREAT. C-CAN'T BREATHE.

"I didn't know you WERE moving," Chad says.

"I only THOUGHT I was," I jabber happily. The words tumble out of me as I relate the whole story.

For a second—don't laugh!—I think I might faint. My legs feel like they're made of pudding. I lift a hand to my cheek and hold it there as my mind reels in happy surprise. RUBY JUST KISSED ME! Cue the fireworks, people. This is incredible.

"Mind if I sit here?"

Randy shrugs. "It's a free country."

I flop down on the grass. There's a long silence. When he speaks again, he can't hide the bitterness in his voice.

"I guess so," I answer.

"Are you going to put that in your gossip column?"

"READ ALL ABOUT IT!
NATE AND RUBY ARE A COUPLE!
AND RANDY'S A *LOSER!*"

"No," I tell him. "I won't do that."

"What's stopping you?"

Good question. What IS stopping me? Maybe I'm figuring out that there's some stuff you just don't gossip about. Or I could be remembering how Randy saved me from Nolan at the museum. Maybe I just feel sorry for the guy. I don't know.

"We're teammates now," I say finally.

He snorts. "Some teammates. We hate each other."

"Not as much as we used to," I remind him.

He nods, a grin slowly creasing his face. "Yeah, I'd like that. But they'll be tough to beat."

"Thunder," Randy says. He squints up at the dark clouds rolling across the sky. "It's going to rain."

"Good. Bring it on."

CHAPTER

12

The Mud Bowl's not like a holiday that happens at the same time every year. Tradition says it HAS to be played in the rain. So you wait for a real gully washer to come along. And then . . .

Let's set the scene, sports fans: It's Friday afternoon. It's been raining for forty-eight hours. And the thirty-eighth annual Mud Bowl is about to begin.

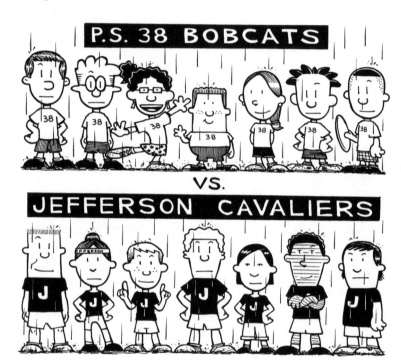

"Wow. They're BIG," Ruby says as we take our positions. She's right. Did Jefferson's whole sixth grade class stay back a year? Or three?

Francis claps his hands. "Let's go over defensive assignments. Dee Dee, you cover the girl with the headband. Teddy, take the kid with the buzz cut."

I shoot my hand up. "I'll take Nolan."

Francis fidgets. "Okay," he says after a long pause.
"We'll see how it goes."

Randy heaves the disk toward Jefferson's end zone, and the game's on.

If you've ever played Ultimate, you know it's pretty simple. The goal is to score points, and you do that by getting the disk into the other team's end zone. But you can't RUN with the disk. You can only score by throwing and catching . . .

. . . which Jefferson's really, really good at.

Cavaliers 1, Bobcats 0. Yikes. That was fast.

Dee Dee leaps around like a deranged cheerleader. "Don't worry, gang! We'll get 'em back!"

But we don't. On our first possession, Randy lofts a high floater in Ruby's direction, and . . .

That makes it 2–0. And minutes later, after Nolan snags another scoring pass high above my head, it's 3–zip. This is a disaster.

Francis turns to the referee. "Time out."

We huddle up. "Let's change a few things," he announces, "before they blow us off the field."

Francis nods. "I know. And he's scored three straight times."

Good thing my face is so dirty. I'm pretty sure that underneath all this mud, my cheeks are turning fire-engine red.

"It's okay, Nate," Ruby says.

"Their whole TEAM'S too tall," Teddy points out.

"Exactly," Francis agrees.

Randy's expression sours. "I thought you guys LIKED the way I throw!"

"We DO . . . but so does Jefferson!"

The game starts up again—with Randy guarding Nolan. I'm still bummed out about getting reassigned, but it doesn't take long to see that Francis was right. Randy's big enough to slow down Nolan's scoring streak . . .

. . . and the mighty Bobcats start chipping away at Jefferson's lead.

They're still taller than we are. (Duh.) But we're quicker and craftier. As the game moves into the second half, we start to creep up on them.

There's just one problem . . . and it's a whopper.

I see what's going on here. And unless I say something, I don't think we can win this game.

I signal to the ref. "Time out."

"Hear that, Bobcats? Huddle up!" Francis calls.

"No," I tell him. "This isn't a team thing."

IT'S BETWEEN ME AND RANDY.

Randy gives me a quizzical glance as we slosh over to the sideline. This could be awkward. I guess the best thing to do is just come out and say it.

YOU'RE THROWING IT TO RUBY A LOT.

His shoulders stiffen. "So? She's a good player."

"Yeah," I explain. "But you're passing to her when she's not even OPEN."

Randy doesn't say anything. But he doesn't slug me, either. Might as well plow ahead.

"Listen, I get it," I say quietly. "You like her."

There's a long pause. He kicks at the ground. "What do YOU know about it? You've never liked someone who didn't like you back."

I gape at him in disbelief. "Uh, HELLO?"

Randy's eyes look a little watery, but that might be because we're standing in the middle of a monsoon. "Whatever," he mutters. "I guess it was crazy, me thinking that Ruby might like me."

"No, it wasn't," I say. "Me trying to play defense against Nolan—THAT was crazy."

The game rolls on. Twice we get to within a point of Jefferson, and twice we fall back. Then, with

less than two minutes to go, Francis makes a sliding catch in the end zone. Tie game, 19–19!

But hold everything. Jefferson gets the disk and starts to motor down the field as time bleeds off the clock. If they score, we might not have time for a comeback. With twenty seconds left, they flip a pass toward the flag . . .

. . . AND NOLAN DROPS IT!!

Randy takes over. He snatches up the disk and turns to me. "GO!" he shouts.

I sprint up the swampy field with Nolan on my heels. We can win this game right now—IF Randy can chuck that disk all the way to the end zone . . .

As I look over my shoulder, I can barely see Randy fifty yards behind me, stepping into his throw with a loud grunt. I peer through the sheets of swirling rain until . . . yes! I spot the disk curving in a wobbly arc toward the corner flag.

BETANCOURT & WRIGHT TEAM UP TO WIN FIRST MUP BOWL IN 37 YEARS

Nicnack Park—For the first few minutes of Friday's epic Mud Bowl against Jefferson Middle School, things didn't look so good for the team from P.S. 38. They fell behind 3–0, and the Cavaliers seemed unbeatable. But after Francis Pope called a time-out for a pep talk, our Bobcats came "roaring" back! (Get it?)

The good guys finally managed to tie the score at 19 with two minutes left, then got lucky when a player from Jefferson dropped a pass. (Ha!)

That's when Randy Betancourt made one of the most incredible throws in sports history, heaving the disk the length of the field to the speedster Nate Wright, who caught it as time ran out.

Speaking of TIME, Jefferson will have a whole twelve MONTHS to lick its wounds! Better luck next year, Cavaliers!

Nate Wright and Randy Betancourt celebrate the victory.

It's been five days since the game, and the whole school's still buzzing about it—especially now that the *Bugle*'s just come out.

"A picture of Nate and Randy hugging," Dee Dee exclaims. "Now that's what I call DRAMA!"

Ruby flips through the newspaper, wearing a puzzled look. "Nate, where's 'Bugle Blasts'?"

"Aw," says Chad as we file into the social studies room. "Now there won't be anything fun to read."

"Oh, yes there will," I announce, pulling a wad of comics from my notebook. "Remember, I'm still the greatest cartoonist at P.S. 38! And this new 'Mrs. Godzilla' adventure is my best ever!"

Lincoln Peirce

(pronounced "purse") is a cartoonist/writer and *New York Times* bestselling author of the hilarious Big Nate book series (www.bignatebooks.com), now published in twenty-five countries worldwide and available as ebooks and audiobooks and as an app, Big Nate: Comix by U! He is also the creator of the comic strip *Big Nate*. It appears in over four hundred U.S. newspapers and online daily at www.gocomics.com/bignate. Lincoln's boyhood idol was Charles Schulz of *Peanuts* fame, but his main inspiration for Big Nate has always been his own experience as a sixth grader. Just like Nate, Lincoln loves comics, ice hockey, and Cheez Doodles (and dislikes cats, figure skating, and egg salad). His Big Nate books have been featured on *Today* and *Good Morning America* and in the *Boston Globe*, the *Los Angeles Times*, *USA Today*, and the *Washington Post*. He has also written for Cartoon Network and Nickelodeon. Lincoln lives with his wife and two children in Portland, Maine.

Also available as an ebook.